PRAISE FOR
THE JASMINE TOGUCHI SERIES

THREE JUNIOR LIBRARY GUILD SELECTIONS

FOUR CHICAGO PUBLIC LIBRARY'S BEST OF THE BEST BOOKS

AN AMAZON.COM BEST CHILDREN'S BOOK

TWO NERDY BOOK CLUB AWARDS

AN EVANSTON PUBLIC LIBRARY'S 101 GREAT BOOK FOR KIDS

A BANK STREET BEST CHILDREN'S BOOK OF THE YEAR

AN AMELIA BLOOMER LIST TITLE

A CBCC CHOICES LIST (BEST OF THE YEAR)

A BEVERLY CLEARY CHILDREN'S CHOICE AWARD NOMINEE

A 2021 NUTMEG BOOK AWARD NOMINEE

A ROMPER'S 100 PROGRESSIVE BOOK FOR CHILDREN

A CYBILS AWARD WINNER

A MARYLAND BLUE CRAB YOUNG READER AWARD WINNER FOR
TRANSITIONAL FICTION

"In this new early chapter book series, Florence introduces readers to a bright character who is grappling with respecting authority while also forging her own path. Vuković's illustrations are expressive and imbue Jasmine and the Toguchi family with sweetness . . . This first entry nicely balances humor with the challenges of growing up; readers will devour it."
    —*School Library Journal* on *Jasmine Toguchi, Mochi Queen*

"Adorable and heartwarming."

    —*Booklist* on *Jasmine Toguchi, Mochi Queen*

ENJOY MORE ADVENTURES WiTH
JASMINE TOGUCHI

JASMINE TOGUCHI
BRIDGE BUILDER

BRiDGE
BUiLDER

DEBBi MiCHiKO FLORENCE PiCTURES BY ELiZABET VUKOVIĆ

FARRAR STRAUS GIROUX • NEW YORK

Farrar Straus Giroux Books for Young Readers
An imprint of Macmillan Publishing Group, LLC
120 Broadway, New York, NY 10271 • mackids.com

Our books may be purchased in bulk for promotional, educational, or business use. Please contact your local bookseller or the Macmillan Corporate and Premium Sales Department at (800) 221-7945 ext. 5442 or by email at MacmillanSpecialMarkets@macmillan.com.

Library of Congress Cataloging-in-Publication Data
Names: Florence, Debbi Michiko, author. | Vuković, Elizabet, illustrator.
Title: Jasmine Toguchi, bridge builder / Debbi Michiko Florence ; pictures by
    Elizabet Vuković.
Description: First edition. | New York : Farrar Straus Giroux Books for Young
    Readers, 2023. | Series: Jasmine Toguchi | Audience: Ages 6–9. | Audience:
    Grades 2–3. | Summary: When Jasmine and family visit Kabo, the Japanese village
    where her grandmother grew up, she is homesick and angry with her older sister
    for not playing with her, but when they start to compromise, they discover ways
    to bridge their differences. Includes author's note and instructions on how to make
    a folding fan.
Identifiers: LCCN 2022047064 | ISBN 9780374389369 (hardcover)
Subjects: CYAC: Vacations—Fiction. | Family life—Fiction. | Sisters—Fiction. |
    Compromise (Ethics)—Ethics. | Japan—Fiction. | Japanese Americans—Fiction. |
    LCGFT: Novels.
Classification: LCC PZ7.1.F593 Jac 2023 | DDC [Fic]—dc23
LC record available at https://lccn.loc.gov/2022047064

First edition, 2023
Book design by L. Whitt
Printed in the United States by Lakeside Book Company,
Crawfordsville, Indiana

ISBN 978-0-374-38936-9
10 9 8 7 6 5 4 3 2 1

TO MY MOM, YASUKO
HIROKANE FORDIANI,
AND IN MEMORY OF MY
GRANDMA MISAO HIRAI AND
YANAGIHARA OBAACHAN,
FOR WONDERFUL CHILDHOOD
SUMMERS IN KABO —D.M.F.

FOR ENDLESS
SUMMER DAYS,
PLAYING IN THE
NEIGHBORHOOD,
EPIC BICYCLE RACES,
AND FANTASIZING
OF TRAVELS —E.V.

CONTENTS

JASMINE TOGUCHI
BRIDGE BUILDER

PARADiSE

I stared out the window of the bus. We drove over a big bridge. I loved bridges. They connected one place to another. They were high up so you could see far-off things.

I looked down. Below us was the ocean. My big sister, Sophie, did not like being up high. It made her nervous. Next to me, she kept her eyes closed and listened to music on Mom's phone. Sophie said it was a good distraction.

We were spending most of our summer

vacation in Japan traveling. We took a plane from our home in Los Angeles to Tokyo. From Tokyo we took a super-fast train to Hiroshima to visit our grandma. Usually Obaachan comes to our house for New Year's and stays a whole month. This was our first time visiting her in Japan. We've been on subways and taxis and even a ferryboat. And we've done a *lot* of walking. Now we were on a bus.

I, Jasmine Toguchi, was on my way to a village called Kabo on an island called Suo Oshima. Obaachan grew up here before she moved to the United States. When Obaachan moved back to Japan though, she moved to Hiroshima. Her sister still lived in Kabo. Mom used to spend her summer vacations here. It was strange to think of Obaachan and Mom ever being my age.

"How much longer until we get there?" I asked Obaachan, who was sitting in front of us.

"We are almost there, Misa-chan," she said, calling me by my Japanese middle name.

I did not really believe her because Dad always said the same thing whenever we were driving some- where. "Almost there" always felt like forever.

Hiroshima
Suo Oshima
Tokyo
Kyoto

Kabo

I looked out the window again. After we crossed the bridge onto the island, the bus drove on a road right next to the ocean. The sun bounced off the sea, making little diamonds on the water. It was very pretty. It was almost like watching a movie.

The bus slowed down and came to a stop. I followed Mom and Dad, Sophie and Obaachan off the bus. After the bus driver unloaded our luggage, he drove away, leaving us in a small shelter.

"Where are we?" Sophie asked.

Across the road was a low wall.

"Go ahead," Dad said. "Take a peek."

Even though the road looked like a highway, there were no cars. Sophie took my hand. We looked both ways, then scurried across.

"Wowee zowee!" I said, leaning on the wall.

Below us were giant concrete blocks, a small sandy beach, and a big blue ocean. It was strange to see a beach with no people on it. Back home in Los Angeles, when we went to the beach, it was always crowded. People sat on towels and beach chairs and blankets. Kids

played catch with balls or Frisbees. Families flew kites, built sandcastles, and waded in the ocean. Surfers rode the waves. It was busy and loud.

Here it was empty and quiet. Peaceful.

Mom came over and put her arms around our shoulders. "Beautiful, isn't it?" she said. "I came here almost every summer when I was a kid. We always had the whole beach to ourselves."

It was like a paradise. Our very own paradise!

"Can we play on the beach?" I asked.

"Yes, but later," Mom said. "Let's go to the house. Your great-aunt, Yasuko Obaachan, is waiting. I haven't seen her in over ten years."

We crossed back to the bus stop. Dad and Obaachan were already walking away on a path, dragging their suitcases.

"We have to walk?" I asked. We walked a lot in Japan!

"It's not far," Mom promised.

Sophie and I grabbed our suitcases and followed Mom. We walked past a school. It had a huge yard.

"They have seesaws!" I shouted.

I have been wanting to ride a seesaw ever since I saw one at a park in Hiroshima. It looked like a long plank of wood with handles on both sides. You and a friend sat on opposite sides and went up and down.

"Sophie," I said, "will you ride with me?"

Sophie scrunched her nose. She did not like to be up high. I looked for Dad, but he and Obaachan were already far ahead of us.

I walked with Mom and Sophie, wishing Dad had waited for us.

"What is that?" I asked, looking down next to the path. Pointing is rude in Japan. I did not point, but  mostly because one hand was dragging my suitcase and the other hand was holding Fred Just Fred. Fred Just Fred was my second-favorite stuffed flamingo. I had to leave Felicia Flamingo at home because she is just as tall as me and would have been hard to carry around.

"These are rice paddies," Mom said. "This is how rice is grown."

I squinted at the field. The area was

flooded with water, and narrow green plants sprouted up.

"It doesn't look like rice," I said.

Sophie screeched next to my ear. I jumped in surprise. Mom grabbed my backpack so I didn't tumble into the rice paddy.

I turned to glare at my sister. "You almost made me fall!"

But Sophie didn't hear me. She was already running away. She flailed her arms around her head, screaming, "A giant bug!"

NOISY NATURE

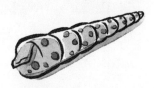

I ran after Sophie. She had already caught up to Dad and Obaachan. I did not want her to get to the house before me.

"Matte!" I called out to her, telling her in Japanese to *wait*. I did not speak Japanese, but I knew some words. Sophie studied before we came to Japan, so she understood Japanese better than me. I was learning new words every day though.

It was very hot and sticky in Japan. I was

hot and sticky, too, by the time I caught up to Sophie at the top of the steep path. There was another narrow pathway that led to a house. Obaachan was talking to someone who looked almost like her. She wore a tan dress with a blue apron over it. She had short gray hair like puffy clouds. Black wire glasses perched on her nose, and her smile was wide, making her whole face light up like the sun.

Obaachan waved us over. "Hina-chan, Misa-chan, this is my sister and your great-aunt, Yasuko Obaachan."

Sophie and I bowed.

Mom and Dad finally caught up. They all laughed and talked very fast in Japanese. Their words skittered and skipped as their voices blended together.

"Doesn't Yasuko Obaachan speak English?" I asked quietly.

Dad patted my shoulder. "She's lived in Japan for so long without visiting the States

that she has forgotten most of her English. Obaachan talks with you both a lot. And she stays with us, so she gets to practice more often."

I took a deep breath. "It smells like oranges," I said.

Mom nodded to the area below us. "It's a tangerine grove. This island is known for their mikan."

"Wowee zowee!" I said. There were so many trees! "Can I climb one?"

Back home, Mrs. Reese, our neighbor, lets

me climb her apricot tree whenever I want. I use it as my thinking tree. I missed climbing and thinking.

"It's better that you don't," Mom said. "These trees are precious. Yasuko Obaachan grows and sells mikan. It's her job."

Sophie nudged me. "That means don't touch the trees, Squirt."

Squirt was the special name Sophie had for me when we were younger, when we were friends. All through her fifth-grade and my third-grade year, she was bossy and mean and ignored me a lot. But since we got to Japan, Sophie has been nicer. She started calling me Squirt again. Sophie and I were getting along and it made me happy! We were going to have so much fun together in Kabo!

We followed Yasuko Obaachan into the house. There was a dirt floor with a raised wood platform just like at Obaachan's house in Hiroshima. I knew what to do. I took off my shoes and climbed up into the house. The adults put on slippers, but Sophie and I stayed in our bare feet. The whole house had tatami floors. They looked like woven straw mats.

Yasuko Obaachan gave us a tour of the house. It had three main rooms: the eating area with a low table, a mostly empty room where we would all sleep, and another room where Yasuko Obaachan slept. Just like at Obaachan's house, all the doors slid open and shut. They reminded me of the doors that slid open to the backyard at my best friend Linnie Green's house. Except her doors were made of glass and you could see through them. The shoji doors here were made of wood and paper, and you could not see through them.

Thinking of Linnie made me miss her. We had never been apart this long. Good thing she gave me a journal before I left. I wrote in it like I was talking to her.

The house also had a kitchen, a bathroom,

and a bathing area. It had a Japanese bath-tub just like at Obaachan's house. You take a bath outside the tub, splashing water on yourself.

We all sat down on zabutons, or cushions, at the low table. We snacked on crunchy cookies and drank hot tea.

At first Mom or Dad would tell me and Sophie what everyone was saying, since they were talking in Japanese. But after a while, Mom and Dad forgot to translate. I had no idea what was going on. I got bored as soon as the food was gone.

Sophie and I walked to the front room. The doors to the house were all slid open. It was like the house had no walls. We could see all the way down to the ocean, where we had gotten off the bus.

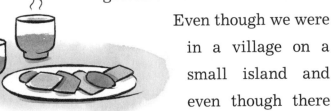

Even though we were in a village on a small island and even though there was no traffic or crowds of people, it was very, very loud.

"What is that noise?" I asked.

"Dad said insects." Sophie wrapped her arms around herself and shivered even though it was hot.

"Whoa," I said. "Those insects must be huge to make such loud sounds. Let's go explore!"

"Um." Sophie looked around the room. "I have to go to the bathroom!" she said as she rushed away.

I sat down to wait. My legs dangled over the edge of the house. I was not surprised Mom was so happy, chattering away with the family, but I also wished she noticed that I was sitting here alone.

Suddenly I heard Sophie scream. I jumped up and ran back to the other room. Sophie dashed in, her eyes wide.

"What happened?" Mom asked.

"There's a frog in the bathroom!" Sophie's face was red.

Obaachan smiled. "There is a lot of nature here."

Sophie grumbled and stalked over to her backpack, pulling out her book. She sat with her back to the wall and read.

I guessed we weren't going to explore after all.

Jasmine's Journal

Dear Linnie,

Konnichiwa! That's hello in Japanese, but I already told you that before. We are finally in Kabo.

I have great plans for adventures here! I want Sophie to explore with me and to ride a seesaw with me. We will go to the beach, and Sophie and I can make sandcastles and play in the ocean. It's a good thing Sophie and I are friends, because Mom is very busy paying attention to Obaachan and Yasuko Obaachan.

But Sophie is reading now. I have nothing to do, so I am writing to you. If you were with me, we could play!

What are you doing today? I wish you were here.

MISSING HOME

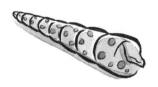

After I finished writing in my journal, Sophie was still reading, so I wandered back to the table. The food was all gone, but now the table was piled with books. I loved books!

I sat next to Mom. "What are you reading?" I asked.

"We're looking at pictures," she said. "These albums have a lot of photos of me when I was your age."

Mom opened a book and pointed to a picture of a little girl in a dress with a strawberry print.

Her hair was in two braids. She was smiling and had a missing tooth.

"That's you?" I asked.

"That's me," Mom said.

"Wowee zowee!"

At first it was fun to see Mom as a kid. There she was lying on a beach towel. And there she was sitting on the steps to this house. There she was eating at a table with some friends. She sure sat a lot.

I had a hard time sitting still. It took forever to turn a page in the album. For every picture, Mom or Obaachan or Yasuko Obaachan had a long story to share. And they kept talking in Japanese and Mom and Dad kept forgetting to translate into English for me.

After a whole bunch of pictures of people I didn't know, I got bored. Again.

I went back to the room where Sophie was still reading. I hugged Fred Just Fred and that made me feel a little better.

I sighed. Sophie didn't hear me. I sighed louder. Really loud.

Sophie finally looked up from her manga. "What's up, Squirt?"

"Let's do something," I said.

"There's nothing to do here," Sophie said. "Mom will take us to the beach tomorrow."

Tomorrow was forever away! I wanted to do something today. Now!

I didn't feel like reading. I didn't feel like playing by myself. I just wrote in my journal, so I had nothing new to say.

I took Fred Just Fred and sat at the front door. Alone and away from everyone who was having a good time. I was happy that Mom was happy, but I was lonely. I thought this vacation was all about family time and being together. But the adults were busy talking and Sophie was reading by herself.

"I miss Linnie," I said to Fred Just Fred. "I bet you miss Felicia Flamingo."

Fred Just Fred and Felicia Flamingo usually shared a spot on my bed at home. Thinking about my bed made me think about my bedroom. Thinking about my bedroom made me think about my house in California.

I wondered what Daruma, my pet fish, was doing. I usually talked to him a few times a day. Linnie was feeding him while I was away. But she only went to my house once a day. Was Daruma lonely? Did he think I wasn't coming back?

We were halfway through our vacation. We had spent two days in Tokyo and five days in Hiroshima. We were here in Kabo for three days and then we were going somewhere else for three more days. I counted on my fingers. Ichi, ni, san, shi, go, roku, six more days until we went home.

Six more days until I was back in my bedroom.

Six more days until I could climb Mrs. Reese's tree.

Six more days until I saw my friends again— Linnie, Daisy, Tommy, and Maggie.

"I want to go home," I whispered to Fred Just Fred, hugging him tight.

HUNTiNG

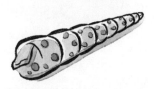

I was glad when it was lunchtime. The adults finally stopped talking.

Yasuko Obaachan grilled fish that came right from the ocean. We ate rice and pickled vegetables and one of my favorite things in the world—umeboshi. Umeboshi is a pickled plum that is sour and salty. Sophie thinks they are too sour, so she never eats them. More for me! I popped the whole thing into my mouth and my lips puckered so much

that Mom and Obaachan laughed. That cheered me up.

After lunch, the adults opened more photo albums. Why?

"Jasmine," Mom said, "come here. I want to tell you a story about when I was your age."

"No thank you," I said. I had enough of stories I couldn't understand. Plus, Mom and I were nothing alike. When she was my age, she wore dresses and her hair in braids. She sat around and didn't do much of anything. Kind of like Sophie.

I did not want to look at old pictures anymore. I wanted to have an adventure.

I joined Sophie in the front room.

"What are you doing now?" I asked.

Sophie waved her manga at me. She did not stop reading.

"Let's go for a walk," I said. "Or we can ride the seesaw!"

"I'm reading," Sophie said. "I'm almost done. This book is really good!"

All this time I wanted to be friends with Sophie. Now that we finally were, I was starting to see that Sophie was not very interesting. She didn't want to play or have adventures. Kind of like Mom as a kid.

"Hey, Jasmine," Dad said, squatting next to me. "Ready to go exploring?"

I jumped up and shouted, "Hai!"

"Sophie?" Dad asked.

I knew her answer before she said, "No thanks."

I liked to read as much as the next person, but we were in Kabo! We would only be here for three days. I wanted to see things. I wanted to *do* things!

Before we could leave the house, I had to put on sunscreen and bug spray. Dad made me wear a hat. I wanted to get outside! But I knew if I complained, it would take even longer, so I did everything Dad asked me to do.

Once we finally had our shoes on, I followed Dad around the side of the house. Two nets with long handles were propped against the wall.

"Are we going fishing?" I asked.

"Not quite," Dad said. He handed me one of the nets. "Come this way."

I followed him behind the house to a bunch of tall trees. "Do you hear that?" he asked.

"I hear a lot of sounds," I said.

Dad laughed. "Yes, nature can be loud. That high-pitched humming you hear is a cicada, or semi in Japanese. When I was a boy and came to Japan to my aunt's house in the countryside, we would catch semis."

That sounded exciting! "What did you do with them?" I asked.

"We kept them in little cages," Dad said. "But we are not going to do that. It's better for them to be free instead of kept as pets."

I nodded. "Like flamingos."

Flamingos are my favorite animal in the world. They are big and pink and tall and loud. They make me happy just looking at them.

"Exactly," Dad said. "It's fun to look for semis and try to catch them. We will set them free right away."

I wasn't sure what we were looking for, but I felt like a brave explorer with my hat on and the net over my shoulder.

"Look, Jasmine!" Dad pointed to a tree.

"Wowee zowee!" I said. "It looks like a giant fly!"

If Sophie were here, she'd scream and run away.

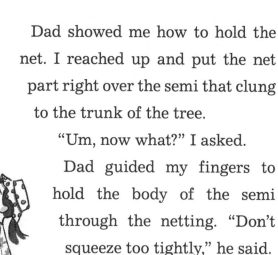

Dad showed me how to hold the net. I reached up and put the net part right over the semi that clung to the trunk of the tree.

"Um, now what?" I asked.

Dad guided my fingers to hold the body of the semi through the netting. "Don't squeeze too tightly," he said.

The semi's body was hard. I did not squeeze too tightly and I tugged it gently off the bark of the tree with the net still around it. I put the insect on the ground. Dad spread the net out so I could see the semi better.

"It's almost as big as my hand," I said.

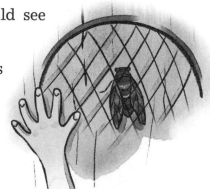

"Pretty cool, right?" Dad said. "These insects live as wingless nymphs underground. When they emerge, they climb a plant or tree. Then they hatch out of their skins with wings, looking like this. Kind of like when a caterpillar becomes a butterfly."

I peered at the insect. "You are very special," I said to the semi.

Dad lifted the net and we watched it fly away.

"Let's look for some more," I said.

Dad smiled and let me lead the way.

Jasmine's Journal

Dear Linnie,

Today Dad and I were hunters! We caught big insects called semis. I wanted to bring one back to show everyone, but Dad reminded me that Sophie would get upset.

She is not very much fun. All she does is read and wants to be left alone.

I miss you. I miss everything about Los Angeles and home. Dad said that is called being homesick. That is when you miss your home and it aches in your chest and tummy. He said it is okay to feel that way. It just means you love your home and your friends.

I wonder if you miss me as much as I miss you?

WAITING IS HARD

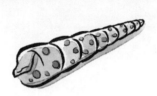

The first thing I saw when I woke up was a big net hanging over me. It made me feel like a bug in a net. Like the semi Dad and I caught yesterday. But actually this net was more like a tent that protected us from mosquitoes while we slept as a family on the futons. Futons were mattresses that unfolded onto the floor. It was fun sleeping all together.

But when I looked around, I was alone.

"Hey!" I shouted. "Where is everyone?"

"Don't be so loud, Squirt," Sophie said from the other room. "We're right here at the table."

I peeked out. Everyone was eating breakfast.

"Why didn't anyone wake me up?" I asked with a frown as I joined my family.

"We thought it would be nice to let you sleep in," Mom said. "It's vacation after all."

I yawned and stretched. Last night the loud buzzing and humming and chirping made it hard to fall asleep. Maybe it was good that I got to sleep in. Today was a big day!

"When do we leave for the beach?" I asked.

Mom served me toast and marmalade. Soft-boiled eggs and sausage. Yum!

"Not for a couple of hours at least," Mom said.

A couple of hours! That was a very long time away!

"Can I play outside after breakfast?" I asked.

"As long as you stay near the house," Mom said.

After we ate, Mom made me brush my teeth and wash my face. I had to help put away the futons. Finally it was time for me to explore.

"Let's go for a walk," I said to Sophie.

Sophie scrunched her nose. "No thanks. I heard how you and Dad caught giant bugs."

"We don't have to catch them or even look

at them," I said. "We can just walk under the trees."

"It's hot out and I hate getting sweaty," Sophie said. She sat in front of an electric fan and let it blow on her. "I'm going to read."

"You said you finished your book last night."

"I did," she said with a smile. "This is book two!"

Walnuts! Sophie was no fun. If Linnie were here, she would walk with me even if she didn't want to see any insects. If Daisy, Tommy, and Maggie were here, too, the five of us would have a blast.

"How about we play hide-and-seek inside the house?" I asked. I really wanted to go outside, but I would compromise if it meant Sophie would play with me. Ms. Sanchez, my third-grade teacher, taught us that compromise was when you met halfway with another person to make an agreement.

"Nope," Sophie said, opening her book. "I just want to read until it's time to go to the beach."

That was not compromising. I looked around for Mom, but she was laughing with Yasuko Obaachan. Just sitting and laughing. Everyone liked to sit.

I wished I was on vacation with my friends instead of my family. They would be more fun.

I scooped up Fred Just Fred, put on my shoes, and went outside. Alone! I did not know why I wanted to be friends with Sophie in the first place.

I showed Fred Just Fred where Dad and I had walked yesterday. I told him about semis.

"They are not little shrimp like you eat though," I said to him. The tiny shrimp flamingos ate helped make their feathers pink.

I scanned the trees and counted—ichi, ni, san, shi, go—five semis on the trees.

But after a while I got bored counting

semis. I went to the mikan grove. The tangerines were still green but were almost the size of the kind we ate at home. Mom said these were not ripe yet and would taste sour. They wouldn't be ready to pick until fall. We would be long gone by then.

I hugged Fred Just Fred as I walked through the grove. It smelled like delicious orange juice. My mouth watered. I wanted to eat mikan. I put Fred Just Fred into the crook of one of the branches. Seeing him in the tree

made me miss climbing Mrs. Reese's apricot tree back home.

These mikan trees were perfect for climbing. The branches were low enough for me to reach. I glanced around. I was completely alone. A little voice in my head reminded me that I was not supposed to touch the trees. But I wasn't going to hurt them. I would be super-careful.

TREE-CLiMBiNG EXPERT?

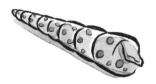

I've had a lot of practice climbing trees. I was a tree-climbing expert!

I reached up and grabbed a low branch. I swung my legs over and lifted myself into the tree. I stood, balancing on the branch. Easy! There was another limb above my head. I reached for it with both hands. I would climb even higher!

But when I tried to lift myself up, the branch sagged and shook.

Crack!

Crash!

I was back on the ground. Fortunately I hadn't been very high up, so I did not hurt myself.

"Jasmine Toguchi!"

I yelped.

Mom ran over to me. "Are you okay?" she asked, kneeling to check my arms and legs. "Does anything hurt?"

I shook my head. When Mom was sure I was not bleeding, she stood and put her hands on her hips. Her forehead wrinkled, and I knew I was in trouble. Would she tell me I couldn't go to the beach? But the only reason I was out here was because no one

would play with me. Mom just didn't understand me.

My heart pounded like a taiko drum.

Boom! Boom! Boom!

"Jasmine Toguchi, you scared me! First I
couldn't find you, and then I saw you fall out
of a tree!" Mom's voice was shaky, like she
was really scared.

"I'm sorry," I said, rubbing the toe of my
shoe in the dirt.

"I told you not to climb the mikan trees,"
Mom said, sounding frustrated.

I burst into tears. "I'm sorry! I ruined
Yasuko Obaachan's trees and now she won't
be able to grow mikan and sell them!"

"Oh, Jasmine!" Mom wrapped me in a hug.
"You didn't ruin it. This tree will still be able
to grow tangerines."

I sniffled against Mom's shirt.

Mom pulled away and looked at me. "Do
you know what I did when I was a little older
than you?"

Oh. Mom was going to tell me stories again about when she was a kid. I already knew we were not alike.

"I climbed one of these trees," Mom said.

That surprised me. It was hard to imagine Mom climbing trees, and I had a really good imagination.

"I fell, too," Mom said. "But I fell from higher up and broke my arm."

"Whoa."

"It really hurt." Mom scrunched her nose like she felt the pain again. "The closest doctor was an hour's drive away. And then I had to wear a cast for the rest of the summer. I couldn't climb or swim or do much of anything. It made for a pretty miserable vacation."

I could almost picture Mom, my age, climbing this same tree. "Did you love to climb and explore?" I asked.

She smiled at me. "I did! I was a tree-climbing expert, just like you, Jasmine."

Wowee zowee! Mom was more like me than I thought!

Mom took my hand, grabbed Fred Just Fred out of the tree, and walked me back to the house. "I'm glad you didn't get hurt, Jasmine. When I make rules, I do it to protect you."

"Gomen nasai, Mom." I apologized again as

I took my shoes off and climbed back into the house.

"Please help Yasuko Obaachan pack the bento for our picnic."

"Our picnic for the beach?" I asked.

Mom nodded.

"I can still go?" I asked.

I clapped my hands over my mouth. *Walnuts!* If Mom had forgotten to punish me, I did not want to remind her.

Mom raised her eyebrows. "Do you want me to say you can't go on a picnic?"

"No way!"

She laughed. "I think falling out of the tree was punishment enough. Just try to follow my rules, okay?"

"Hai!"

Jasmine's Journal

Dear Linnie,

Guess what? I helped Yasuko Obaachan make a bento lunch for a picnic.

We made omusubi. You've had those rice balls before at my house, remember?

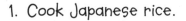

Here is how to make omusubi.

1. Cook Japanese rice.

2. Scoop rice into a bowl so it will cool off enough to touch it.

3. Wet your hands with water. Sprinkle your hands with salt. Try not to get salt everywhere (says Mom).

4. Take a handful of rice.

5. Put something yummy and bite-size in the middle. I like umeboshi, but you can also put cooked meat or even vegetables in the middle.

6. Form a ball around the food. It's like playing with your food and not getting in trouble!

7. With dry hands, wrap the rice ball with a strip of nori (dried seaweed). When you eat the omusubi, you can hold the nori part so you don't get rice all over you.

Now we are going to the beach. I wish you were here. Then we could play and eat bento together.

BEACH DAY

"Be careful," Mom said.

She helped me and Sophie through the narrow opening in the low wall so we could get to the beach. First we had to climb over big concrete blocks. They were like an obstacle course of bridges, helping us get from the street to the ocean.

"What is with these things?" Sophie asked, holding on to Dad's hand.

"These blocks protect the land from being washed away by the waves," Dad said.

"It's like a fun playground," I said.

Sophie screamed and I almost fell off a block.

"A creepy crawly!" Sophie shouted. She climbed into Dad's arms even though she was too big to be carried.

"I'm not sure what they're called, but they're harmless," Dad said, holding Sophie.

I scrambled over to where Dad stood. "I want to see," I said.

"There's one." Mom pointed down by my feet.

It looked like a giant pill bug, gray with scales that looked like armored plates. "It's like a little dinosaur," I said. "Cool!"

"It's gone now, Sophie," Dad said, setting Sophie back down.

She held on tight to Dad as they slowly picked their way over the blocks.

I scurried over the concrete and ran to the sand. "I win!" I cheered for myself.

I jumped up and down. I hopped on one foot and then the other. I had a lot of happy energy! We were finally having a fun family day at the beach.

Mom, Dad, and Sophie caught up to me. We had the whole place to ourselves. Mom and Dad put towels on the sand so we could sit. I blew up a floaty ring. Sophie checked a towel, probably worried about bugs, before she sat down.

"Aren't you going to blow up your float?" I asked her in between breaths.

"Nope." Sophie curled her legs under her so she wasn't touching the sand at all.

I pressed my lips together so the angry words wouldn't fly out. Instead of having fun adventures, Sophie stayed in the house reading. Now she wasn't going to swim in the ocean? What a waste of vacation. I would have fun on my own. I did not need Sophie!

"Come on, Dad," I said, hugging my floating tube.

Dad scooped me up. I screamed. Not because I was scared, but because I was happy and excited. I bounced in Dad's arms as he ran into the ocean. The warm water splashed my legs.

I laughed as we went deeper. I felt safe with Dad. When he stopped, the water was past his tummy. My legs felt all floaty and light in the water.

"Whee!" I shouted as a wave splashed us. "Okay, Dad, put me down. I want to swim!"

I climbed through my floating tube and kicked my feet, spinning in the water. Dad and I paddled and swam. My hair and face got wet and salty. The water was so clear I could see my toes as I touched the sandy bottom.

"Look, Dad!" I said.

Tiny silver fish darted left and right, swirling around in a group. If Sophie saw this, she'd probably scream and leave the water.

"Lunchtime," Mom called from the beach.

I was very hungry! When I flopped down on the towel next to Sophie, she yelped.

"You're all wet," she complained.

I moved to sit with Mom. Sophie raised her eyebrows at me. I think she was surprised I didn't say anything to her.

We ate omusubi, tamago, and edamame.

Best of all, Mom let me eat with my hands (after she wiped them clean with a towel).

Sophie bit into a rice ball. "You did a good job with the omusubi, Squirt."

I did not answer her and just ate my lunch. Quietly.

After our picnic, I said, "Let's build sand sculptures, Dad. Mom can be the judge."

While Dad and I scooped and smoothed our creations, Mom invited Sophie to be a judge with her. *Walnuts!*

I mounded wet sand into two islands. Then

I connected them with a stick I had found on the beach. "It's a bridge," I said. "I'm on this island and, Dad, you're on that one. Now we have a bridge so we can be together."

"I like that, Jasmine," Mom said.

Dad made a turtle out of sand. He was super-cute.

Dad and I ended up in a tie. Mom voted for my creation and Sophie, of course, voted for Dad's. I was not surprised.

"It's too sunny," Sophie complained. She put her hand over her eyes.

Dad opened a beach umbrella, and he and Sophie sat under it in the shade. Boring. I looked over at Mom. She was scooping sand onto her bare feet and humming to herself. She probably wanted to just sit there, too. But then I remembered that she used to be an expert tree-climber. Mom as a kid was a lot like me.

"Do you want to do something, Mom?" I asked.

"Sure," she said, standing up. "Let's go for a walk. Sophie, do you want to come?"

Sophie looked at me. If I weren't so annoyed with her, I would have begged her to come with us. But I did not say anything. Sophie shrugged and said she'd sit with Dad.

Mom and I walked along the shore, our feet making shadowy imprints on the wet sand. It felt a little squishy, but nice.

"Look, Jasmine," Mom said, pointing down.

Was it another creepy but cool dinosaur bug? There by Mom's foot was something white. I stooped down and picked it up.

"A seashell," I said. It was tiny, the size of my thumb. "It looks like a little doll's bowl."

"Oh, and here's another," Mom said, picking up a pink shell. "It's broken, but it's still pretty."

We kept finding more shells. We collected them until we couldn't hold any more.

"When I was a girl, there were even more

shells," Mom said. "Some as big as your hand. Obaachan kept them and they are in the house."

"Can I see them?" I asked.

"Of course," Mom said.

"I like to collect shells, and so did you when you were my age," I said.

Mom and I smiled at each other. I felt connected to Mom. My heart felt full.

Jasmine's Journal

Dear Linnie,

(Sophie is taking a bath first, so I am writing to you while I wait my turn.)

Here is a list of things I'm good at:

1. Being your friend
2. Tree-climbing (except for falling out once)
3. Mochi-making
4. Collages
5. Flamingo facts
6. Being a pet fish owner and . . . today I added something new
7. Seashell-collecting!

Mom and I found so many shells on the beach just now! Tiny white shells

that look like miniature unicorn horns and spiral snail shells in black and pink and brown. I will bring some home to you!

I wish you were here. Sophie is being boring, but surprise, surprise, Mom is actually a lot of fun!

SHELLS AND SURPRISES

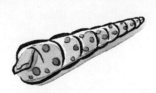

After I finished writing in my journal, Sophie still wasn't finished with her bath. Mom was, for once, not busy. Obaachan and Yasuko Obaachan had gone to the store, and Dad was taking a walk.

"Mom? Can I see the shells?" I asked.

"Let's wait for Sophie," she said. Then she laughed at the face I made. "Okay, I can show them to you now."

That surprised me. Usually Mom was very

strict about being fair when it came to me and Sophie. I smiled, feeling special.

Mom led me to a wall. Except it wasn't a wall but a door. She slid it open and we stepped into a little room I hadn't known was there. Inside was a big shelf at the front of the room. And next to us was a large chest of drawers that looked like steps going up against the side of the wall.

"Don't climb on that," Mom said. "It's an

antique chest called a tansu. It belonged to your great-grandfather."

I learned my lesson from the mikan tree. Even though the chest looked perfect for climbing, I would stay off it.

On each step part of the chest was a shell. "Wowee zowee!" I said. "Those are big!"

Mom picked up a giant snail shell that was green and black on the outside and shiny pink on the inside. She handed it to me. It was heavy.

"What are you doing?" Sophie asked as she stepped into the room. Her hair was still wet from her bath. Her very long bath.

"Mom's got an awesome collection." Seeing all the shells made me forget I was kind of sort of mad at Sophie.

"This is a scallop." Mom handed Sophie a flat brown-and-cream shell with rounded edges. "You may each pick one to take home."

I hopped on one foot twice and on my other

foot three times. I had a lot of excitement energy! There were so many to choose from. I wanted the best one. A weird purple ball caught my eye. I liked it because it was my favorite color.

When I reached for it, Sophie did, too. We frowned at each other.

"Oh, girls," Mom said with a sigh. "There are at least twelve shells and you want the same one?"

"What is this one?" I asked Mom.

"It's a sea urchin shell," Mom said.

I decided I didn't want anything that Sophie wanted. I let go of it and held up the shell in my other hand. "Can I keep this?" It would be special, since it was the one Mom gave me.

"Of course," Mom said with a smile.

Sophie ran her finger along the bumps of the sea urchin shell. Would she snatch it? She looked at me. "Well, if Jasmine can pick another one, I can, too. I will keep the one you handed to me, Mom."

"I'm so glad," Mom said.

"What's that shelf for?" Sophie asked.

"I'll show you," Mom answered. She led us to the front of the room. There were two framed pictures. In front of the pictures were a metal bowl with incense sticks, a plate with grapes and an apple, and a small bowl of rice.

"That's a picture of my dad on the left and that's my uncle on the right, Yasuko Obaachan's husband," Mom said.

I peered at the photos. I had never met Mom's dad because he died before Sophie and I were born. He looked nice. He smiled with his mouth closed, and his eyes were happy and kind.

"What are the bowls and plate for?" I asked.

"This is a home altar to pay respect to family who are no longer with us. You light the incense sticks and you can talk to your family member. We leave food for them, too," Mom explained.

Sophie squeaked. "Like ghosts?" She scurried to the door and clutched her shell.

"No." Mom shook her head. "Not like ghosts. Maybe more like spirits. Friendly spirits."

Sophie, with wide eyes, looked like she was ready to run away.

"It's okay, Sophie," Mom said. "Come back."

I followed Mom back to the tansu. Sophie did not move. I shrugged. Fine by me.

"The tansu holds clothes," Mom explained to Sophie.

That got Sophie to move. She loved clothes. She came and stood beside me.

"Tomorrow we are going to a festival to honor our ancestors." Mom smiled at Sophie. "I want to show you girls something special."

Mom pulled open a long shallow drawer. It was the longest drawer I'd ever seen in my life. I bet I could lie down in it if it were deeper.

Sophie and I leaned forward to peer into the drawer.

DANCE LESSONS

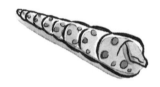

Inside the drawer was a pretty kimono!

"This is a yukata," Mom said. "A summer kimono."

"Wowee zowee!" I said. "It's so pretty!"

"This is the one I wore when I was your age, Jasmine." Mom handed me the yukata. It was white with blue and pink flowers. It felt as light as air. Perfect to wear on hot summer days in Japan. In March, we wore kimonos for Girl's Day. Girl's Day is a Japanese celebration of girls. Those kimonos were heavy and had a lot of layers. Too hot to wear in the summertime.

Mom pulled out another yukata. "And this is the one I wore when I was a little older than Sophie." She handed Sophie a yukata with orange flowers and green leaves.

Sophie held it up in front of her. "What are these for?" she asked.

"Tomorrow night is the Obon festival," Mom said. "It's a special celebration honoring our ancestors. It's thought that our ancestors return to visit us here during this time."

Sophie made a small sound. I was tired of Sophie being scared and not wanting to have adventures. "Mom said it wasn't like ghosts. So don't get scared, Sophie!" I huffed.

Mom and Sophie both gave me strange looks.

"What do we do at Obon?" I asked, ignoring Sophie.

"It's like a big party," Mom said. "We dress up in yukatas and happi coats. Happi coats are shorter than yukatas and you wear your regular clothes under them. Then we gather with the other villagers at the schoolyard. There will be food and music and dancing."

"That sounds like fun!" I shouted. I started spinning around the room. I loved to dance!

Mom laughed. "It will be a little different than that," she said. "It's a special kind of

Japanese dancing. We will head over there in a bit and learn the dances before tomorrow night."

She hugged both of us.

"I think you both will have a lot of fun," she said. "We will all have fun together."

I glanced at Sophie and shrugged. It would be a miracle if I could have fun with Sophie.

After the rest of us took our baths, we walked over to the school that was near the bus stop. The yard was crowded with people. *Wowee zowee!* I didn't even know this many people lived in the village. We hadn't seen anyone since we got here.

"Can we ride the seesaw?" I asked Mom.

"Maybe later," she said. "Come with me."

Walnuts! I really wanted to try the seesaw. Just when I thought Mom finally understood me, she went back to being . . . Mom.

Sophie and I followed Mom to a group of people. There were grandmas and moms and even kids like me and Sophie! I walked up to two girls my age. Finally! Someone to play with! Maybe they would ride the seesaw with me.

"Konnichiwa." I said hello in Japanese.

They smiled at me and started talking in Japanese. Oops. I did not understand them. I smiled and answered in English. "I'm sorry. I don't speak Japanese."

They didn't seem to care. A girl grabbed my hand and pulled me over to another group of girls. One of them said, "Hello. Nice to meet you," in English!

"Hi! I'm Misa," I said.

"Watashi wa Kiku desu," she said.

I figured out that Kiku was her name. And then the other four girls shouted their names. This was fun!

Mom came over and said, "It's time to learn

the dances. Just follow the moves of everyone else."

I lined up with my new friends, facing three women standing at the front. When Sophie came over, the girls all started to talk with her. Sophie understood them and answered in Japanese.

The music started and the women in front began to move. They clapped. I clapped, too. They stepped forward and raised their hands. I kept copying them. Clap, clap. Raise my hands. Pull back.

After practicing our moves, we lined up in a circle.

"We will dance around in a circle tomorrow," Mom said.

Sophie was chatting in Japanese with my new friends. I wished I understood. She was being friendly and having fun with strangers, while she had been boring all day and didn't want to have adventures with me in Kabo.

My face got hot. It was hard to breathe. I heard a roaring in my ears like crashing ocean waves.

The music started up again and now Sophie was in front of me, between me and the girls. We started to move forward. It was hard to dance and walk at the same time. It was hard to remember the order of the dance moves, especially when my anger at Sophie kept filling me up.

I clapped a little later than everyone else. I moved forward when everyone else moved backward. I stepped on Sophie's heel.

"No, Jasmine," Sophie said. "You step forward twice and then backward."

"Stop being bossy," I said a little too loudly.

Sophie stared at me, her mouth

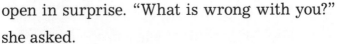

open in surprise. "What is wrong with you?" she asked.

I didn't answer her.

"Wow," she said, peering at me. "Are you mad at me or something? Why?"

"You are ruining everything!" I shouted.

People stopped dancing and looked at me.

Mom said something in Japanese and bowed. Then she took my arm and Sophie's and led us over to the other side of the yard. Away from the dancing.

"Girls, what is going on?" Mom asked. Her forehead was wrinkled. I knew that meant she was not happy.

"Don't ask me," Sophie said. "Jasmine is the one who is all grouchy."

"Sophie is selfish," I blurted out. "She doesn't know how to compromise. She won't play with me. She's boring!"

"You're being rude!" Sophie said loudly. "And you're the one who's selfish, wanting to make me do things I don't want to do!"

"Girls," Mom said. "Please keep your voices down. Coming to Kabo was very important to me. I wanted to share what my childhood vacations were like. I have wonderful memories. I wanted both of you to experience the same. Please, for me, try to get along."

One thing was for sure, I could not get along with Sophie. But I would at least try to be nice because it was important to Mom.

MAKiNG UP

"Ohayo, Misa-chan," Obaachan said. "Come have breakfast."

"Ohayo gozai masu." I said good morning. I sat down next to Obaachan. She and Mom and Yasuko Obaachan had been talking together so much that I had not spent a lot of time with Obaachan in Kabo. That would have been fine because I thought I would be having fun with Sophie, but I was wrong.

Obaachan served me a bowl of fried rice.

I ate slowly. Even though I had slept in, I still felt tired.

Last night I fell asleep right away, without even reading first. Dancing was tiring because there were a lot of steps to remember. But the most tiring thing was pretending to be nice to Sophie when I was super-annoyed with her.

"When do we go to Obon?" I asked.

"Not till dinner," Dad said. "I have to go to the schoolyard to help set up."

"Can I go with you?" I asked.

"Sorry, sweetie," Dad said. "It's only adults right now because we're doing a lot of build-ing and moving things around."

I wanted to argue, but I remembered how Mom said rules were to keep me safe.

"We can do something together," Sophie

said, sitting down next to me. "Whatever you want."

Well, that was a first. I did not remember a time that Sophie let me pick something to do. And this was the first time since we got to Kabo that she wanted to do anything with me.

"Come on, Squirt," Sophie said, nudging me. "You can't stay mad at me forever. You can even show me those weird loud bugs you and Dad caught."

I wrinkled my nose at Sophie and crossed my arms. It was too late for her to try to be my friend.

"I'm going to read," I announced. I picked up *Charlotte's Web*, my favorite book, and sat down in the front room.

Sophie helped Obaachan put away the futons and no one made me help. Normally that would make me happy because I am not a fan of cleaning up. But this time it made me feel a little sad. I stared down at my book. It reminded me of all the times I read with Linnie. I felt homesick again. I hugged Fred Just Fred and maybe I cried a little.

"Hey, Squirt." Sophie sat next to me.

I wiped my eyes on Fred Just Fred.

"I'm sorry I haven't been very good company in Kabo," Sophie said softly. "I was excited about reading my manga in Japanese. And to be honest, all the flying and creeping bugs scared me."

"Plus the frog in the bathroom," I reminded her.

She smiled. "Yes, the frog in the bathroom was a surprise."

"I like frogs," I said. "I wish I had seen it."

"I wish you had, too. I wish it had surprised you instead of me." Sophie patted Fred Just Fred. "Just because I don't feel like doing the same things as you at the same time doesn't mean I don't want to hang out with you. We can be different but still like each other."

I thought about Mom and how I thought we

had been different, but we were really more alike.

"We aren't that different," I said to Sophie. "And we can compromise."

Sophie nodded. "You're right. I could meet you halfway. I could have read my manga to you and told you what it said in English."

"Maybe I could have drawn while you read," I said. "We could have at least sat together."

"I could have played hide-and-seek with you when you asked," she said.

My heart felt funny, like it was aching but in a good way. "Dad said I was homesick."

"I'm sorry you felt that way," Sophie said. "I will try to be a better sister and friend."

"Me too."

Now I really was excited about Obon!

BRIDGE BUILDER

When it was finally time to leave for Obon, Sophie and I were a team. Mom helped us into our yukatas, which was way easier than wearing a snug kimono with many layers. I loved my pretty yukata. Mom put my hair up in a bun with a hair ornament, just like Sophie's. My ornament had origami crane decorations and Sophie's had flowers. We both wore our zori (flip-flops), but Mom wore special shoes called geta. They were like zori but were made from wood. Mom's shoes *clop clop clopped* as we walked to the schoolyard.

When we got there, I shouted, "Wowee zowee!"

The yard looked totally different. There was a raised stage with a giant taiko drum! I knew how to play the taiko. I took lessons at home.

There were crowds of people wearing yukatas and happi coats. Women and girls

had hair ornaments like mine and Sophie's. Other adults and kids wore hachi-maki wrapped around their heads. There were tables set up with plates of food. So much food! The delicious smells made my tummy rumble.

"You two stay together," Mom said. "When the music starts, go over to the drum stand. We will dance around it."

"Hai!" Sophie and I said yes together.

"What should we do first?" I asked. "Eat?! Or maybe find those girls from yesterday."

"I have a better idea." Sophie took my hand.

I made a face. *Walnuts!* She was going to boss me around again. I thought we were going to compromise and be a team.

But then I saw where she was taking me. The seesaw! But Sophie did not like to be up high.

"Are you sure?" I asked.

"I'm sure," Sophie said, gripping my hand tighter. "Just don't go too fast."

We climbed on opposite sides. We hiked up

our yukatas. Good thing we wore shorts underneath.

Slowly we went up and down, up and down. I could see the whole schoolyard. I felt like I was flying! Sophie held on tight to the handle. She smiled, but it did not look like a happy-having-so-much-fun smile. My heart felt full knowing she was doing this just for me, to make me happy.

The seesaw looked a little like a bridge. She was on one side and I was on the other, but we were connected. All it took was a few steps to be together again.

I finally got to ride a seesaw, thanks to Sophie. Now it was time for me to compromise and let Sophie off this seesaw.

"I see Dad," I said. "Let's go eat!"

After we ate a lot of yummy food, the music started. I lined up with Sophie and the other girls to dance. We clapped and shuffled forward and back. My favorite was the dance with the fan. I loved to flutter my fan up and

down and open and close it in time to the music.

"Jasmine," Mom said as she came over to me. "Would you like to play taiko?"

"Hai!"

As Mom walked me to the taiko stand, I remembered that she used to play taiko, too. Mom was the one who told me about taiko drums. Mom liked to climb trees and collect

shells and have adventures, too. And I thought about how Sophie and I liked different things, but we shared things, too. We loved our family and we had a lot of memories together.

Mom helped me up onto the taiko stage, and the man at the drum handed me his bachi. When the music started again, I played the taiko.

Boom, boom, boom!

I looked out over the schoolyard, the same one that Mom used to play in on her summer vacations and now the same one Sophie and I danced in on our summer vacation. I searched the crowd and found Obaachan and Yasuko Obaachan. They were laughing and dancing. The lanterns made bright lines across the yard, like bridges of light.

Memories and experiences were like bridges, connecting all of us together.

Boom, boom, boom! My heart pounded with love and joy!

Jasmine's Journal

Dear Linnie,

Guess what? I got to play taiko at the Obon festival! It was a giant drum much bigger than the one I play for my lessons. It was the best! I got to keep the folding fan that I danced with. I will show you it when I get home.

Here in Kabo I learned that my mom was a lot like me. She has been telling me a lot of stories. I am making a list of all the things she has done that I want to do, too.

1. Swim on a team

2. Bike at the beach

3. Go camping

(And a lot more!)

I was feeling homesick, but now I am feeling happy again. Sophie and I are a team!

We leave tomorrow for Kyoto. Obaachan is coming with us! She is going to show us pretty gardens there. I can't wait!

I miss you! I will be home soon.

AUTHOR'S NOTE

Kabo, Suo Oshima, is a real place in Japan. However, the way I describe it in this book is not the way it is today. I've set this story in the Kabo of my childhood, in the 1970s. Kabo was always a very small village, but the population has steadily shrunk over the decades. According to the 2015 census, there were 243 people and 87 homes in Kabo. As of April 2017, the population of the entire island of Suo Oshima was about 17,000, with only two middle schools and one high school on the island.

My mother spent her childhood from the age of eight months to ten years old living in Kabo in a house very similar to the one Jasmine visits. When I was a child growing up in Los Angeles, we took family summer vacations to Japan often. Every trip we would spend at least a week in Kabo.

My memories are filled with walks to the beach, where my two cousins, my sister, and I floated on blow-up rings in the ocean. We'd collect seashells that I still have today. My cousins and I would catch semis, and my mom's cousin would tie string like a leash around them so we could carry them with us. My cousin who was my age and I used to put our younger siblings in wheelbarrows and race them down the mountainside path from the house, along the rice paddies, to the schoolyard. And one of my favorite memories is of celebrating Obon right there in the schoolyard, just as Jasmine did.

I also have fond memories of participating in Obon odori (Obon dance) in West Los Angeles when I was young. As an adult, I attended Obon in San Jose with my own family.

Obon is a time for remembering ancestors, but it is also a time to gather with friends and family, dance, eat delicious food, and play games in the booths. I hope you will get a chance to attend an Obon celebration. Keep your eye out for neighborhood announcements (usually at Japanese Buddhist temples) in the late summer.

MAKE YOUR OWN FOLDING FAN

Folding fans in Japan have been around since as early as the eighth century. Used in tea ceremonies, dancing, theater, and as art, today they are commonly used by all to cool off during hot days.

MATERIALS

- Construction paper
- Markers
- 3 inches of ribbon or colorful string
- Stapler

INSTRUCTIONS

1. Place the construction paper in front of you with the long side down (horizontally).

2. Using markers, draw a colorful picture or design on one side of the construction paper. It can be anything that makes you happy. Perhaps a beach scene, a favorite animal, or a garden.

3. Turn the paper so the short side is facing you, with your picture facing to the left (vertically).

4. Fold the bottom edge up about one inch.

5. Flip the paper over so the blank side is facing you.

6. Make another fold up, matching the fold you just made.

7. Flip the paper back over so the picture is facing you.

8. Make another fold up. Continue flipping and folding until the entire paper is folded into one narrow (one-inch) strip.

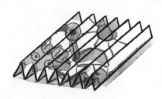

9. Use a ribbon or string to create a loop around one end of the folded paper. This will be your wrist strap, so make it wide enough to fit your wrist. With the help of an adult, staple the folds and two ends of your ribbon or string together about one inch from the bottom of your picture.

10. Spread the top folds to open your folding fan! Enjoy cooling off!

Turn the page for a sneak peek of . . .

JASMINE TOGUCHI

GREAT GARDENER

DEBBI MICHIKO FLORENCE   PICTURES BY ELIZABET VUKOVIĆ

BE SURE TO LOOK FOR
JASMINE TOGUCHI
GREAT GARDENER
COMING SOON!

WiNNiNG
A PRiZE

"Ow! Your bony elbow is in my side," my big sister, Sophie, said to me.

"Well, your knee is jabbing me," I said.

I, Jasmine Toguchi, was having a super summer vacation with my family traveling in Japan! But right now was probably not the best part. I was smooshed in a minivan taxi with Obaachan, Dad, Mom, and Sophie, plus all our suitcases. We had just arrived in Kyoto by train and now were taking a taxi to our hotel.

"Girls," Mom said. She was squished next to me. "Please don't complain. We're almost there."

Mom's shoulder was shoved against my head, but I did not say anything because I didn't want her to be annoyed. Usually when Mom or Dad say "almost there," it still takes forever, but for once Mom was right. The taxi pulled up to a hotel and stopped.

"Quit pushing," Sophie said as she climbed out of the minivan.

"I'm not! Mom's pushing me," I said.

"Girls!" Mom said, while nudging (pushing) me out of the car.

We tumbled out of the taxi, gathered our suitcases, and made our way into the hotel. It was cool and quiet in the lobby. There were big windows everywhere. Through the glass I saw tall bamboo and lots of green leafy plants. It was almost like being outside still. And the best thing was, I was not smashed in the back seat of a car with my family anymore.

I hopped and jumped, excited to finally be at our hotel.

"I'm glad we're out of that taxi," Sophie said to me, stretching her arms.

"And we have three more days of vacation left," I said.

She smiled. "We're going to have a blast here."

Spending time with Sophie has been supergreat! Before we came on vacation, we were not getting along because she was not very nice to me. Now we were friends and having fun together.

While Mom and Dad checked us into the hotel, Sophie and I followed Obaachan to a sitting area. There was a vending machine! I loved how many vending machines there were in Japan. You could buy drinks, candy, toys, and more. This one was the small kind like we had back home, where you put in a coin and spin the dial and get a mystery toy in a plastic ball.

"Would you like to get something?" Obaachan asked with a twinkle in her eye. She knew we would say hai! She gave us each a coin. The money in Japan is called yen. I learned that when we were in Tokyo.

"Who gets to go first?" I asked.

"Jan ken pon," Sophie said.

Whenever we played rock paper scissors, Sophie usually won. It was not very fun for me. We faced each other with one fist forward.

"Jan, ken, pon," we both said, shaking our fists. On pon, I kept my fist closed and Sophie opened hers. She cheered as she covered my fist with her hand. "Paper beats rock. I win!"

Sophie put in her yen and spun the dial. She opened the plastic ball, and inside was a cute key chain in the shape of sushi. I wanted one of those too!

I spun the dial and pulled out a bright-pink ball. I was excited to see what I got. But instead of a cute key chain or toy, inside was a folded piece of paper. I opened it, and on it was Japanese writing. This was not a good prize at all! It was not fair that Sophie got a fun toy and I got paper.

"Oh. This is unusual," Obaachan said, looking at my paper. "It's a fortune."

I peered at the writing. "It is?" That sounded interesting.

"What does it say?" I asked Obaachan.

"It says daikichi. It means a great blessing is coming your way," she said. "Something very good."

Wowee zowee! I wondered what it could be. A special present? A delicious treat? Whatever it was, it would be a good surprise!

Dad walked over to us and held up two key cards. "We have rooms next to each other," he said. "One of you will stay with Obaachan."

"Me, me!" I shouted at the same time as Sophie.

"Jan ken pon?" Sophie asked me.

Again? I wished Dad would tell us that I could be with Obaachan, but I knew that wouldn't happen. This was the only way. We held out our fists to play and I got ready to be disappointed.

"Jan, ken, pon!" Sophie and I said. On pon,

Sophie opened her fist to make paper again. But this time, I flashed two fingers into scissors.

"Scissors beats paper," I said, surprised. "I win!" I hopped twice on my left foot and three times on my right. "This is my great blessing!"

Obaachan laughed. "Perhaps. But I think it will be something even better. Let's wait and see what happens while we're here."

Sophie frowned and I thought she was mad at me for winning. But then she smiled and said, "Fine, Squirt. I guess you get to stay with Obaachan."

Squirt might seem like a mean name, but Sophie only calls me that when we are friends. I like her special name for me. And this meant she was not mad at me for winning.

"Yes!" I hugged Obaachan. She smelled good, like pine trees. "I get to share a room with you."

Mom said to Dad, "Should we be offended that we are not the grand prize?"

I felt a little bad, but then I saw they were both smiling. They were teasing. They knew this trip was special, visiting our grandma in Japan for the first time ever.

When we got to our rooms, Obaachan let me put the key card in to open our door.

"See you in a little bit for dinner," Mom said as Sophie opened the door to their hotel room. Then Mom leaned close to me and whispered, "Please behave with Obaachan."

That was a silly thing to say. Of course I was going to behave!

Jasmine's Journal

Dear Linnie,

We made it to Kyoto! And guess what? I'm sharing a room with Obaachan while Sophie stays next door with Mom and Dad. How did this happen? I won jan ken pon! I also got a special fortune that said something fantastic is going to happen. I can't wait to find out what that is! I'll be sure to tell you when it happens.

At dinner, Obaachan said that Kyoto is famous for its gardens. I'm excited! I love gardens! Remember how we grew beans in Ms. Sanchez's class for a science project? We planted the beans in dirt and watered them. It was fun watching the little seeds sprout

leaves and stems. I can't wait to see all the plants in Kyoto!

Obaachan is getting ready for bed. She will turn out the light soon, so I will write to you tomorrow.

Oyasuminasai! (Good night!)

ALL BY MYSELF

I changed into my pj's and climbed into bed. I got a big bed all to myself! I hugged Fred Just Fred. He was my second-favorite stuffed flamingo. I had to leave my favorite flamingo, Felicia, at home because she was just as tall as me. We do a lot of walking in Japan and it's very hot and sticky in the summer. Carrying Fred Just Fred was easier. And to tell the truth, Fred Just Fred was becoming my favorite along with Felicia. Fred Just Fred and I have made many memories here together.

I fluffed my pillows. I smoothed my blankets. Our room had air-conditioning, so it was nice and cool. I slid into the bed and pulled the quilt up to my nose.

Obaachan stepped out of the bathroom wearing a pretty blue nightgown.

"It feels strange sleeping in a bed," I said to her. For most of this trip, we had slept on futons. Not the foldout-couch kind like in the US, but the Japanese kind—thin mattresses that go on the floor, made up with sheets and blankets that get put away the next morning.

I really liked sleeping on futons with my whole family in one room.

Obaachan got into her bed. There was a big nightstand between us. It made her feel very, very far away.

"Are you ready for tomorrow?" Obaachan asked while she rubbed lotion on her hands. It made her smell like Christmas.

"I'm excited to see the gardens," I said.

"Me too." Obaachan smiled. "It has been a long time since I was last in Kyoto. I'm happy to be here with you."

"This is the best summer ever," I said.

"I think so, too, Misa-chan." Obaachan called me by my Japanese middle name. "Oyasumi."

"Oyasuminasai, Obaachan," I said.

When she turned out the light, the glow from the night-light in the bathroom made the room feel cozy.

I heard Obaachan get comfortable. *Rustle rustle.* I heard the *hmmm* of the air conditioner. I didn't hear Sophie mumbling in her sleep and I didn't hear Dad's soft snoring.

I missed feeling Sophie beside me. I even missed her kicking me in her sleep. I sighed loudly.

"Is something wrong, Misa-chan?" Obaachan asked.

"I'm lonesome," I said, squeezing Fred Just Fred. I hoped I didn't hurt his feelings. He did a good job keeping me company. "It feels strange sleeping all by myself."

Obaachan turned the light back on. "Would you like to sleep with me?"

She didn't have to ask me twice! I scrambled out of my bed, holding tight to Fred Just Fred, and climbed into Obaachan's bed. She tucked the blankets around me and turned off the lamp. I rested my head on her shoulder. This was much better.

Obaachan's hand smoothed my hair and kept rubbing my head gently. My eyes got heavy. I felt safe.

Have you joined Jasmine on all of her adventures?
Check out these other stories featuring your favorite bridge builder!